THE WIND BLEW

THE WIND BLEW
PAT HUTCHINS

Aladdin Paperbacks

Aladdin Paperbacks
An imprint of Simon & Schuster
Children's Publishing Division
1230 Avenue of the Americas
New York, NY 10020
Text copyright © 1974 by Pat Hutchins
First Aladdin Paperbacks edition, 1993
Printed in Hong Kong
20 19 18 17 16
The text of this book is set in Korinna, with the display set in Quaint Open.
The illustrations are full-color tempera paintings.

Library of Congress Cataloging-in-Publication Data
Hutchins, Pat, date.
        The wind blew / Pat Hutchins.—1st Aladdin Books ed.
            p.   cm.
        Summary: A rhymed tale describing the antics of a capricious wind.
        ISBN 0-689-71744-X
        [1. Winds—Fiction.   2. Stories in rhyme.]   I. Title.
    [PZ8.3.H965Wi   1993]
    [E]—dc20   92-44903

For Mark

The wind blew.

It took the umbrella from Mr. White
and quickly turned it inside out.

It snatched the balloon from little Priscilla
and swept it up to join the umbrella.

And not content, it took a hat,
and still not satisfied with that,

it whipped a kite into the air
and kept it spinning round up there.

It grabbed a shirt left out to dry
and tossed it upward to the sky.

It plucked a hanky from a nose
and up and up and up it rose.

It lifted the wig from the judge's head
and didn't drop it back. Instead

it whirled the postman's letters up,
as if it hadn't done enough.

It blew so hard it quickly stole
a striped flag fluttering on a pole.

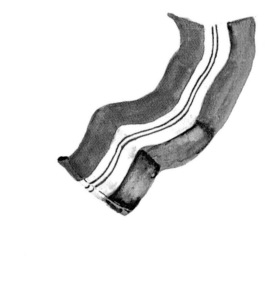

It pulled the new scarves from the twins and tossed them to the other things.

It sent the newspapers fluttering round,
then tired of the things it found,

it mixed them up

and threw them down

and blew away to sea.